Within Gallows Reach

by

Mila A. Ballentine

PUBLISHER'S NOTE

This novel is a work of fiction told from the perspective of fictitious character experiences. The names, places and characters are products of the author's imagination. Any resemblance to actual persons living or dead, business establishments, event or locals is coincidental.

For Tiffany

From Tabitha's lips...

∞

"I am the defiler of worlds, the bearer of imminent death." -Tabitha O'Brien

Prologue

Near the pond's edge, Tabitha's scarlet gaze shifted from the bale of turtles idling on a rock and traveled to what lay beyond the tenebrous waters, which was shadowed by a gathering of trees. For miles debris lay about the wasteland, ramifications of the officious wave that had come ashore and wedged large debris in their limbs. This was a far contrast from their last visit. Back then, a green meadow greeted them, but the current condition prompted her to reflect on what life was like after they first came to Draíocht Dol.

Tabitha's heart sank, knowing fully well that they'd survived under dire circumstances, and yet all else paled in comparison to what lay ahead. Tears slipped from her eyes just knowing it had come to this—coping with the loss of her husband, Marc, and youngest son, Jon, but thankfully she wasn't alone. Her eldest, Uri, stood beside her, immersed in a timid midafternoon light.

As she turned away from the pond and walked to the wagon, the wind disturbed threads of her raven hair. Uri trailed her, reflecting on his greatest transgression. *Had I known, I could have prevented his death*, he thought on the verge of tears, and his body tensed as he recalled what happened that day.

Tabitha's hair fluctuated in color and flowed backward without the benefit of the wind, her flesh rippling as she unleashed her fury—a cantankerous brew of deadly sins which harvested a belligerent tectonic wave, battering everyone and everything within a 60-mile radius.

From then on, a skin crawling sensation took hold that quickly intensified, but by then he'd caught up with her. Now they walked side by side, hand in hand, only for him to let go seconds later to pass a hand along the mare's neckline. Tabitha mounted and positioned herself in the seat of the wagon. Uri climbed the opposite side, sat beside her and flapped the reins, which sent the horses cantering down the road.

As they drove away, the turtles they'd observed earlier scuttled onward, their nails gripping the rock until they dove into the contaminated pond, where just below the surface lay a weight filled with copious amounts of gaseous mixtures.

1

Upon entering their yard, Uri parked at the side of the house and helped Tabitha down from the wagon. A few feet ahead of her an obscure figure came into view as her feet met the ground. From then on, vague features refined, creating a precise rendition that brought Tabitha to her knees, a fitting stance for someone wallowing in self-pity and sparring with bouts of regret.

Almost immediately, she found herself engaging in a conversation—even though she was the only participant. "It can't be," she murmured, and yet it was—her deceased son, Jon, running toward her open arms. By the time he arrived, his rendering dissipated just as a rush of cold air passed through her, immediately changing her temperature from normal to a cryptic chill.

Noticing her distress, Uri asked, "Are you o…"

"Did you see him?" she cut him off, anxiously staring ahead with a stunned look in her eyes.

Clueless as to what she was referring to, he remained tight-lipped. Tearful, Tabitha turned to him. "I'm fine—really," she replied to his initial question.

His body tensed as he observed her. "Your ... your eyes," he said, pointing at her. "They're bleeding." He nervously gazed at her and stumbled but then quickly regained his footing, all while his heart beat tumultuously in his chest.

Puzzled by his skittish demeanor, Tabitha touched her eyes and lowered her hand only to find it tarnished with blood. "It's probably nothing," she said though unconvincingly. "There are more important matters to worry about."

Despite what he'd witnessed, the last thing Uri wanted to do was upset her further, especially since he'd recently made amends for his costly mistake. "You're right." He helped Tabitha to her feet and then peered at the remains of their home.

While the O'Briens made plans to reconstruct their home out in the heart of the badlands, where they last visited, the gaseous compounds continued to accumulate, which ultimately roused submerged remains from the lakebed to the surface.

2

The O'Briens sifted through the debris, reclaiming what wood they could find that lay about the land and stacked it, while an older couple on Vermouthshire began their day at Rebecca's Teahouse. By now, a uniformed server who was a young woman with youthful features and long, shimmering, dark hair, approached a table and greeted them accordingly.

"Good morning, Mr. & Mrs. Finkelsteen." She placed a cup of tea on the silk table dressing in front of the tall, slender man with bushy blond hair, and put the other in front of his spouse.

"I'll let you know how *good* the morning is when I'm through," he grumbled. His wife, Margret, a woman who could easily pass for dead, traced her index finger along the fresh flowers set in a bronze vase at the center of the table. She looked at the server and smiled, causing the wrinkles at her outer eye to congregate. "Pay him no mind. That will be all for now, dear."

Mr. Finkelsteen, a regular of the eatery, though not by choice, also frequented the Social Nomad, an upscale bar on Lick Liver Drive, but for the time being he put up with his wife's socialite tendencies. For a woman of diminished means, she made sure they got out of the house each day.

Even though it was morning, the booze he so often wore like cologne made the server nauseous. On the verge of gagging, she left their table and went on to tend to another customer two tables ahead.

Mr. Finkelsteen lifted the cup, brought the rim to his lips, and peered curiously out the window while Margret admired the head dressings of the women in the room. Since their tea arrived, a line had formed outside. On the other side of their window, women dressed in elaborate clothing, coupled with broad, extravagant hats or embellished bonnets, shielded them from the brunt of the sun. You'd think they were waiting to get into the popular eatery, but you'd be wrong. They were waiting for Dorcas's Haberdashery, the store next door, to open.

Around town, men jokingly referred to the store as *Samson's Bane*. What Delilah achieved by relieving Samson of his hair, the women who shopped there achieved by spending their husband's money on whatever their hearts desired.

Margret's eyes returned to him as she spoke, "There's been a lot of chatter about the missing residents of Clod Hill."

Mr. Finkelsteen nodded. "Be careful, you never know who is listening." He played with his curled mustache while making a mental note of the people within listening distance.

Margret sighed wearily, "Yes, I'm well aware of that. Have there been any developments?"

"None whatsoever." He sipped the tea and placed the cup on the saucer.

Based on the conversations within eavesdropping distance, she wasn't the only one with questions, but what was more troubling was the fact that no one seemed to have an answer to that question. So naturally, residents came up with scenarios of their own and they spread like wildfire.

13

As word spread about the disappearance of Donovan Kingsley, a news article circulated stating that no trace was left of the mansion on Clod Hill, which was a disturbing aspect in and of itself.

At least on Draíocht Dol, imprints of everything that ever existed remained, and yet, what most would consider a natural occurrence after a flood—the fragrance of lingering death—converted the fresh air into a petulant fetor as a swollen cadaver turned onto its side, revealing a botched head and a permanent foggy gape.

3

The Vermouthshire police department had a high profile case on their hands, so they assigned the case to one of their finest. Detective Hunter Sloane was the top recruit in his graduating class and thanks to his hound dog instincts, and relentless determination he was the first promoted to detective. It had taken eight years, but he'd earned the respect of his peers and yet remained humble. Though to be fair, his comrades made a point of bringing up his accomplishments every chance they got. "With no cold cases to speak of, he's simply the best at what he does," someone said.

"That's because I'm here to work, not play hopscotch like you jokesters," he quipped.

To date, Donovan Kingsley's case was the most notable he'd had. In fact, he had just finished interviewing a list of prominent business owners that had dealings with him. Other than that, Detective Sloane couldn't account for any of Kingsley's staff, so he sought other means of obtaining information. Nearly all of Kingsley's employees were men: Leonard, the butler who was widowed; and 2 single men in their 20s, except for the cook who was a middle-aged woman. Sloane played with his pencil. *What do men with plenty of cash and lots of free time do? Drink their way to the bottom of the barrel or empty their pockets entertaining women?*

Strumming the surface of the desk with the pencil, he sat there contemplating what to do. Afterward, he drove away from the one-story clay brick structure that was located less than a mile from the town center, and made a left on Lick Liver Drive as he passed the Social Nomad - which now filled the black Ford's rearview mirror.

A mile out from the downtown area, he sat idling in the lane as he looked at a building across the street. The honk of a horn brought his attention back to the road; he looked in his mirror and saw a car behind him. Sloane pulled off the road and parked. A short walk later, he entered *Decadence of Lustful Delights*, an upscale brothel.

Madame Chevaliéa seductively swayed her hips as she strode cunningly towards him.

"Good afternoon. Do you have someone specific in mind … a type?" the pale, voluptuous woman with hooded eyes and fiery red hair asked with a sultry purr.

Her gaze climbed his body as he stood there staring blankly ahead. The peach bustier dress she wore smothered her bosom into compliance; the middle slimmed her waistline, and the rest of her garment curved against her hips like a second skin. Sloane looked on with disinterest and displayed his badge. "I'm Detective Sloane. I have some questions for you."

His words caused her to lose interest in him. "I can't imagine why you'd want to question me." Madame Chevaliéa placed a hand on her chest and sighed while he looked around the lobby.

"You'd be surprised how helpful you can be. Do you have any clients that work for well-to-do families?"

"It's highly likely, but the girls would know more about that than I would. Besides, what they discuss during pillow talk is confidential—no different from a lawyer-client privilege agreement."

He furrowed his brows. "I doubt that. Do you know if any of your clients worked for Donovan Kingsley?"

"We might have catered to a few over the years, but most recently there was a young man who courted three of my girls."

Court a harlot? Detective Sloane fought the urge to chortle. "Are they here? I'd like to have a word with them."

"Sure. Follow me. You can use one of the rooms. Questioning them in the lobby might spook the customers."

Madame Chevaliéa escorted Detective Sloane to a room normally used for lovemaking. He spoke at length to Abigail and Lyla, but the conversations they held with their clients weren't particularly useful to the investigation. Immediately thereafter, he spoke with the third courtesan, Penni, in a room farther down the hall. Within the confines of the room - which reeked of heavy perfume and perspiration, she divulged all of her activities.

Three months prior, Anton Newman, Kingsley's guard lay limp in a bed with an attractive, bell-shaped courtesan in his arms. On the wall facing the foot of the bed, an oil painting depicted women with their breasts exposed and their lower extremities draped in textiles. Anton reached for a bottle of wine on the small dresser near the bed, drank straight from it, and then gave it to her.

Penni raised a brow as she read the label. "What's the occasion?"

Newman leaned into her and groped her left breast. "I got a new job—and I wanted to celebrate with my favorite gal," he said and kissed her roughly on the cheek.

"Congratulations lover boy, but what's in it for me?" she asked and sat up in bed with the sheet gathered at her midriff.

"Regular visits!" Newman flashed her a wink. Anton looked up at the ceiling and considered the cost of working for Donovan Kingsley. *He pays well, but there's no telling what he'll have me do.*

"Mhmm." Penni swung her leg over his; straddling his hips as she leaned in for a lustful kiss.

She was about to go into the unabridged details of her sexual escapades with Anton when Detective Sloane, his face getting redder by the second, stood up. "That's all I need to know."

Penni ogled him while she wantonly played with the string on her top, twirling it around her finger, loosening the laces one by one. "What's the rush?" She seized his hand. "You're more than welcome to stick around, and spend some time with me," she said seductively sliding her fingers over the top of her bosom. "I'll make it worth your while."

"Not for all the tea in China. But if you think of anything that might help with the investigation, give me a call," he took back his hand and gave her his card.

While Sloane wrapped up his visit to the brothel, a final act of defiance was taking place on Draíocht Dol, as the corpse lying on the surface of the pond exorcised a final gasp, freeing a fume from its twisted lips, filling the area with the malodorous smell. A splotched, murky brown hue—unlike the living—an abnormal transformation that gave the cadaver an otherworldly appearance as if helium filled the body, distorting its features enough to inspire nightmares and even more so when the floater writhed.

4

After concluding his conversation with Penni Cromwell, Detective Sloane traveled down the hallway to the reception area where Madame Chevaliéa leaned against the host's desk. He jotted notes down on his pad and tucked it in his pocket.

"I'll be on my way."

"Pleasure-wise, you can come back anytime," she said, eyes traveling the course of his body.

He shook his head, walked out, and drove back to the station. During the ride, he shrugged off an unsettling thought that came to mind … perhaps he could say that it was a symptom of the profession, but over the years, Detective Sloane harbored distrust for his fellow citizens. In his eyes, everyone was a suspect; they were guilty until proven innocent – even when the law said otherwise. Comments like, 'he or she would never do that,' irked him. What most fail to realize is that everyone has an unconscionable doppelganger hidden just below the surface, waiting for an inopportune moment to strike. And based on what he'd learned thus far about Mr. Kingsley, he considered him to be one of the shrewdest, most unscrupulous characters he'd dealt with thus far.

Oddly, they'd first met when Mr. Kingsley filed a missing person's report for his son. At that time, Donovan Kingsley came across as cold and uncaring; he didn't display the signs you might expect from a concerned parent, beyond reporting him missing. After having been missing for several years, Albert Kingsley was presumed legally dead, which gave his father the leeway to collect life insurance at his son's expense. Unfortunately, Albert's body still had not been found.

Naturally, in his line of work he'd dealt with all sorts of characters, seen the worst in the best of them, and came to the conclusion that some people live veiled lives, consciously displaying the traits they want others to see while they conceal the dark aspects of their personality. Yet, somehow those closest to them remain oblivious to their true intent. Not to mention those brave souls who come to their defense, because admitting otherwise would mean that they'd been deceived. Oftentimes, those in question are the ones who lend a helping hand with yard work, would bring your groceries to the front door, or even babysit your kids. Though to be fair, no one would credit Mr. Kingsley with the former or the latter.

As he drove through the business district, it came to mind—*all roads lead to this boulevard. So, someone had to have seen something.* Detective Sloane drove past specialty shops flanked by Royal Poinciana trees. Midway through the block, a line of mostly middle-class homemakers and tailors of the well-to-do stood outside Dorcas's Haberdashery. After making a U-turn, he parked half a block away, walked to the haberdashery and stood in line. Detective Sloane cleared his throat; a woman ahead of him in line looked back at him.

"Is the line usually this long at this time of day?"

She sighed softly. "It never fails. It's tiring, but it's worth the extra effort."

"That's good to know. Thank you." He stepped out of the line. "May I have your attention please," he said in an authoritative manner and displayed his badge, prompting everyone in line to look in his direction. "I'm Detective Sloane." He put the badge away. "By now, I presume you've all heard of Donovan Kingsley—a wealthy businessmen who's gone missing," he paced, eyeing them like a drill Sergeant. Whispers erupted halfway through his announcement. "People don't vanish without a trace. Someone had to have seen or noticed something out of character. He was last seen approximately ten days before the flood." After an about-face, he went down the line again. "So, if you saw anything suspicious or unusual around that time, please step forward."

Two women stepped out of the line. He approached an older woman standing further ahead. Detective Sloane towered above her ornate hat, so she lifted her chin to make eye contact with him.

"What did you see?" he questioned.

Her nose elevated, she said, "I was waiting in line when a vagrant had the *audacity* to go down the line begging us for money. Are the days of waiting peacefully outside a shop without being harassed gone?"

Detective Sloane sighed. "When you consider the fact that not that long ago a flood devastated our sister island, Draíocht Dol, I'd say it's the least of our worries. Not everyone is as fortunate as you and I. Many have lost everything, so I'd expect that sort of thing to happen until conditions improve."

She huffed. "I sure hope not," she tightened the grip on her purse.

"If that's all, I'll move on." He mumbled something under his breath and he walked on to a flaxen-haired woman standing in a slightly arched stance, rubbing her protruding belly.

"Did you see anything that struck you as odd during that time?"

"Yes... I did, but I wasn't in line at the time. I was on my way here when I came across a couple, covered in guts and blood," she said, but softly, as if she were telling a deadly secret.

A tingling sensation traveled throughout his body as the fine hairs on his arms stood upright. "Where were they going?"

"That way—toward the waterfront."

The unsettling awareness transcended well beyond Vermouthshire's shores to Draíocht Dol where a stale, briny breeze combed through the land near Turtle Pond, mingling with a cantankerous stench—far worse than the smell of a decaying animal at the side of the road. An odor so foul it stayed with you regardless of any measures taken to rid yourself of the scent. Logically, there was no reason why the blood-splotched remains that had long returned to the depths of the lakebed to find its way back to the surface again, and yet strangely it did. The deflated corpse's browning, gray-black skin gradually regenerated, lightening to a murky, lively pink before settling into a pale, ash white hue. Yet the putrid odor remained.

5

Uri finished stacking the containers in the shed and then contemplated their newly rebuilt home, which stood amid the barren landscape like a beacon of hope. The sharp sound of the hoe's blade making contact with a stone drew his attention out to the field where Tabitha worked the soil. Sweat dampened wisps of her hair and left the fine baby hairs at her hairline clinging to the side of her face in a serpentine manner. As she caught her breath, their eyes met in a glance. She smiled at him and went on with her chore.

Shortly thereafter, he went over to her and placed a hand on her shoulder. "We've done enough today. You should rest."

Undeterred, Tabitha went on with her task.

꙳꙳꙳

After digging up some information on his own, Sloane felt like his brain had gone through a grinder. Regrettably, his probing wasn't as fruitful as he'd hoped, and now he had to decide whether to pass the statement he obtained from the expecting woman at the haberdashery on to another officer or handle it himself. However, while he was listening to her revelation a knot formed in his throat, but it wasn't the only sensation that surfaced. Right after he'd spoken to her, an unsettling feeling developed in the pit of his stomach that failed to subside. Considering all that he'd learned, every aspect of the case defied logic, but its peculiar nature kept him curious, even though he had yet to obtain any direct leads that could account for Donovan Kingsley's whereabouts.

6

As the boat edged toward the mooring, Sloane leapt onto the landing, even though they had yet to secure the vessel to the berth.

"Hey," the boatman yelled at the top of his voice, "try that shit again, and it will be the last time you ride on this boat." Unfazed, Detective Sloane displayed his badge and hustled onward.

A man sitting beneath a tree near a wagon caught his eye; he jogged over and introduced himself, after which he bartered a price. In no time, they were on their way, navigating bumpy roadways, shielded from the stifling heat by adjoining trees.

"Is it usually this hot?" Sloane dabbed his forehead with a handkerchief.

"It depends …" the driver who introduced himself as Dudley, said while working the reins. "Sometimes we experience four seasons in a day," he said as he steered the wagon into the yard.

Uri heard the trot of horses entering the yard as he hunched planting seedlings near a grove of trees and stood erect. Soon after, Tabitha noticed him walking over to a fair-haired fellow stepping down from the wagon, but she stayed put.

"Good day, I'm Detective Sloane." He extended a hand and Uri shook it.

"I've already spoken to the other residents. Now it's your turn. I'd like to speak with the man of the house regarding the disappearance of Donovan Kingsley."

Uri's hands moistened. "That would be me."

Detective Sloane's lips formed into a trite grin as he eyed Uri. "You've heard of him, haven't you?"

"I have, but I only know as much as anyone else. He's been in the paper a lot lately. News travels fast, even in a place like this."

At that instant, a thought came to mind and Detective Sloane ran with it. "Have you ever visited Vermouthshire?"

"Yes, but it's been awhile."

"Really ... how long ago was that?" he inquired further.

"Sorry—don't keep track of that kind of stuff. Like I said, it's been awhile."

"Well, there's a couple that was last seen in the downtown area that I'm curious about."

"I doubt I'll be of any use on that subject."

"I'll be the judge of that. The couple in question boarded a boat to Draíocht Dol," Detective Sloane added while his eyes shifted to the open door. "A dark-haired woman accompanied by a fairly handsome young man with blonde hair from what I've heard ... perhaps he's her nephew or son. It's unclear at this point what they were doing, but they were covered in blood," he said coolly as if they were discussing the weather. "They were seen in the shopping district prior to their departure." Detective Sloane scratched the crown of his head.

A shrug of the shoulders was all his elaboration garnered from Uri. Weary of his evasion tactics, Detective Sloane sighed. "We'll speak again." He briefly glanced over Uri's shoulder. "Is the lady of the house in?"

"She's over there," he pointed her out in the field.

"Thank you," Detective Sloane wound his way through the path to her location, and soon his shadow encompassed her. Lowering his gaze, Detective Sloane noticed a dark, red stain on the border of the slip worn beneath her dress.

"Good afternoon. I'm Detective Sloane from the Vermouthshire Police Department. You seem busy, so I'll try not to take up too much of your time."

She didn't stop what she was doing. Sloane gritted his teeth. He needed to look them in the eye, especially during questioning. It helped him to size them up, but Tabitha stood with her back to him.

"Yes, I am. Why are you here?"

"I've been assigned to a missing person case. Donovan Kingsley's to be exact. Do you know him and have you or anyone else in your household had any business dealings with him?"

"I know of him, but personally, I haven't dealt with him, although he was interested in doing business with my husband."

Detective Sloane's eyes brightened. "Was that your husband back at the house?"

Tabitha released an irksome breath. "No. That's my son."

"Is your husband here?"

"I wish it were so, but he perished in the flood." A single tear soiled her cheek. "In a perfect world, I wouldn't outlive my husband or youngest son. I would know when it was to rain beforehand, and also know the best time to plant to assure a bountiful harvest, but outside of using a Farmer's Almanac, no one is afforded those luxuries, detective. No one." Then, she turned sideways without meeting his gaze, giving him the opportunity to notice her moistened cheek getting redder by the second.

Saddened, he submitted to her, "I'd be lying if I said, 'I know what it feels like to lose someone,' but I'm sorry for your loss." An uncomfortable silence lingered before he continued. "Based on eyewitness accounts, his disappearance seems to coincide with an odd couple that chartered a boat to Draíocht Dol."

At that point, the blade of the hoe hit a stone; Tabitha hunched downward, removed the pebble, and tossed it aside.

"When was the last time you visited Vermouthshire?" he asked.

"Two years ago, when the Lavinia docked to let off passengers," she said, continuing to guide the tool.

"I see. I should head back now. Thank you for your time."

Sloane strolled back to the wagon and encountered Uri standing nearby. Unbeknownst to him, Uri sneered on the inside, even as he displayed a blank expression while he eyed him intently.

"I'll be on my way," Detective Sloane said and nodded as he stepped up and positioned himself in the seat next to Dudley.

Uri nodded as well. "Safe travels." He strode over to his mother. "Should we be worried?"

Tabitha locked eyes with him. "Not at all. He's angling, but we're not biting." Mother and son stood side by side and looked on as the carriage promptly traveled out of the yard, leaving a trail of dust behind.

7

"If you'd stayed any longer, you'd be walking back to the wharf," Dudley said, jittering as he glared briefly at him sideways.

Sloane turned to him. "Why?"

"I brought that family out here when they first came to Draíocht Dol. At first glance, they appeared to be normal until I saw *those inhuman things* she calls eyes. So, if I were you, I wouldn't return."

"I didn't see her eyes, but she seemed ordinary enough."

A short time later, the wagon parked near the dock.

"Thank you, sir." He was too preoccupied to notice before, but now he took note of Dudley's emaciated face and macabre gaze as he paid the fare. Then, Sloane hoofed it to the end of the boardwalk, and during that time he reflected on Dudley's spiel about Mrs. O'Brien being something other than human—it was by far the most absurd thing he'd heard to date, especially given the fact that Dudley didn't look all that great himself. Detective Sloane chortled, shook his head and boarded the ship.

❧❧❧

On the way into the precinct, Detective Sloane bumped into his overseer, Sergeant Eddie Pistone. Eddie's single eyeglass popped off the perch of his nose. He caught his eyeglass and put it in his shirt pocket. "Have you found out anything useful?"

"It's too early to tell, but I'll keep you posted," Sloane tensed his jaw.

Pistone sighed, "All right, carry on."

8

Detective Sloane greeted his fellow officers on the way in, sat at his desk and wasted no time getting to work. Less than an hour after his arrival, a petite young woman stood outside the entrance, inundated with sweat due to walking from the countryside to the police station. After several minutes had passed, she caught her breath, entered and scanned the room. Detective Sloane happened to look up as she looked in his direction. Golden locks spilled unapologetically alongside her oval face and even glistened as they caught the sunlight. He gestured his hand for her to come; she came over and stood at the front of his desk.

"Can I help you?"

Astrid wiped tears from her eyes with a bloody handkerchief. "I hope so."

"Please, have a seat." She sat in front of his desk with a dire look in her eyes.

He eyeballed her, waiting for her to say something. It took a while, but she did. It turned out that Astrid, the otherworldly woman seated before him, was Donovan Kingsley's assistant cook who'd returned from an extended absence of caring for her ailing mother. Only hours earlier, she had discovered that the Kingsley's mansion was gone. She was visibly shaken after he explained what had happened since she had taken her leave.

However, hours earlier, she had ambled up Clod Hill while cooling herself off with a handheld accordion fan. Arriving at the top of the hill, she turned in place and tried to make sense of her surroundings. *Did I take the wrong route*? she asked herself. *It should be over there*, her line of sight went to where the mansion that formerly overlooked the valley sat. "It can't be—it should be right here. I've walked this path too many times," she said aloud.

Even though it was hot outside, her body temperature dropped drastically within milliseconds, sending her frame into a trembling frenzy. Her eyes widened as she observed her breath clouding the air.

Astrid clasped the pendant on her chain with a sense of urgency and clenched her eyes. Her hold tightened around the cross as she muttered a prayer, so much so that it drew blood that trickled down the center of her wrist.

She had no information to share concerning Donovan Kingsley's whereabouts, but she shared details of the crooked business dealings he engaged in and when she was through, she heaved a sigh.

"Are you okay?" Detective Sloane asked.

"I'm a bit tired, that's all."

"I can have an officer take you home, if you like."

"I'd appreciate that. Thank you."

"DK—you busy?" Sloane asked.

Detective Dutch Kershaw's nose slightly rose from a book. Unlike Sloane, he was a poor excuse for a cop. His aggressive and occasional brash behavior made suspects go out of their way to avoid him. For all intents and purposes, Detective Kershaw accepted his status, but with simmering disdain. He looked Detective Sloane square in the eye and then went back to reading the book. As exhausting as it was, he'd developed contempt for Detective Sloane's successes, even though they were best mates throughout the training period up to now.

"Take her home, please. You owe me one," he said simperingly.

DK rubbed the back of his neck as he got up and strolled over. "When you say it that way, I can't refuse." Dutch escorted Astrid to the entrance.

So far, the investigation into Donovan Kingsley's disappearance proved to be more challenging than he'd anticipated, and yet he had a feeling his luck had changed.

As Detective Sloane gloated, Astrid broke free from Detective Kershaw and sprinted to Sloane's desk, wild-eyed and panting. "There's something amiss in these lands, both fierce and vengeful, and I can assure you," she added, "that it will leave nothing but destruction in its wake." By any account, her accusations were irrational - and yet - the stern look in her eyes said otherwise.

Unamused, Detective Sloane stared at her without saying a word. If only she'd kept her 'crazy' under wraps, at least for the time being, he could take her seriously, but after that display, not even a grain of salt could save her.

9

"So much for that," Detective Sloane said quietly as DK escorted her outside. He stared briefly at the names she'd jotted on the back of a scrap of paper, stored it in the drawer and ventured outdoors, passing Barney's Hardware store as he walked the footpath.

"From what I've heard, this product works wonders, especially during the dry months," Sloane overheard. In passing, he acknowledged them and continued down the path. Astrid provided details about matters Detective Sloane wasn't privy to. Most of his staff with the exception of two other workers—the butler, housekeeper, main cook, and the driver—lived on-site in the help's quarters. Additionally, he learned that Mr. Kingsley's assistant and guard lived in the rooms for rent downtown.

Come to think of it, he wasn't that far from the building, so he walked to the location and came across a young man smoking outside. "Excuse me—do you know where I can find Anton or Bryson?"

"Never heard of them." He dragged on his cigarette and blew smoke in Detective Sloane's face. "Ask Billy. He's the second door on the left. That nosy bastard knows everybody."

Detective Sloane coughed as he fanned the smoke away and entered the building. He went a short distance down the hall and knocked lightly on the door. A balding man with a row of checkered brown teeth opened the door wearing nothing but his boxers and a dingy white vest.

"Sorry to bother you, but I'm looking for Anton, a short, stocky guy."

"You're out of luck. He's no longer with us—he died during the flood. It's in the newspaper; you should try reading it sometime." Billy moved to close the door.

Detective Sloane wedged his shoe between the doorframe. "How about Bryson; have you seen him? He's a tall fellow with blond hair and blue eyes—the light kind—keeps to himself."

"He went by that name at one point, but not anymore. He goes by a different name now, but I can't remember at the moment," Billy said snapping his fingers as if by doing so his name would come to him. "Damn it. I know it—Uri! That's it. The last time I saw him, he was hightailing it out of here and Anton was chasing him. That was before the flood, of course."

A tinge of excitement came over him, "Thank you. You've been more helpful than you know." Sloane unwedged his foot from the door, traveled down the narrow hall and walked back to the precinct.

10

"I'll start looking for work," Uri said as he sat at the dining table. Tabitha stood.

"Yes, that's a great idea," she said and carried the dishes to the kitchen, but then she turned and faced him. "Once we get back on our feet, I'd like to reopen the shop."

"Father would love that," he said wearily. An abrupt knock on the front door halted their conversation. Uri went over to the door, "Who is it?" Having received a reply, he opened it. "I thought we'd seen the last of you."

"Not yet," Detective Sloane began to pace just outside their front door.

"Couldn't this wait until daylight?" Uri griped.

"Maybe—maybe not, but either way, I'll be the judge of that. When I first came here …" Detective Sloane paused and then continued, "… the couple I mentioned before, the older woman traveling with a young man ..."

Uri picked at his finger as Detective Sloane spoke.

"… Out of all the residents, only you and your mother fit that bill."

Uri looked at him. "They could have come from somewhere else or perhaps the information you obtained is flawed."

Tabitha came to the door. "Aren't you going to invite Detective Sloane in?" she asked while shielding her eyes from the glare of the fading sun.

Uri didn't bother to answer her. Tabitha looked over the detective's shoulder, "Where's your ride?"

"Down the road," his brows arched and then relaxed.

"Oh ... come in."

Detective Sloane brushed against Uri as he entered. Uri went off to the side, toed his boots off and laid back on the bed, but kept an eye on him.

"We have leftovers. Would you like me to fix you a—?"

"Yes, thank you."

"Have a seat." She fixed him a plate, set it in front of him and sat beside him. As their eyes met, he detected her delicate features. Her eyes were gentle—nothing out of the ordinary. Clearly, Dudley had a flair for the dramatic, which hindered his credibility.

"Is there something else you'd like to know?" She smiled briefly as she poured him a drink from where she sat.

"Yes, I'm trying to locate a young man by the name of Bryson who worked for Mr. Kingsley."

Uri sat up in bed, "What do you want with him?" he asked.

"I'd like to have a word with him."

"I am he."

Sloane's face tensed as he bit down on his inner lip. "The last time we discussed Donovan Kingsley, you made it seem like he was insignificant—come to find out that you worked for him. What else are you keeping from me?"

"At the time, I failed to realize the importance," Uri's nostrils flared as he sighed. "I was his personal assistant."

His admission heightened Detective Sloane's curiosity. "I went by that name because I had no idea who I was at the time, but once that changed, I quit."

"Ah, I see." Detective Sloane's posture loosened. Satisfied with his rebuttal, Detective Sloane turned his attention to Tabitha and reverted to small talk. "How's the harvest?" Sloane scooped generous portions of food onto his fork.

"Most of the seedlings will die before the drought is over."

"Is there a way to prevent that?" he asked, wrinkling his forehead.

"Outside of doing a rain dance, and wetting the crops with rationed water, there isn't much we can do."

Sloane drummed his fingers on the surface of the table. "I'm sure something will work out."

"I hope so."

He wiped the corners of his mouth and put the napkin aside. "Thank you. Dinner was lovely, but I must go. I'll be on my way now. The boat waits for no man," he said and walked to the front door.

"Take care," she said, observing him as he rushed out the door and down the path.

11

Halfway down the road, Detective Sloane realized that Dudley was gone so he continued on foot. A mile into the trek, he looked up at the sky and whistled the rest of the way as the sun sank in the horizon. He stopped whistling when he realized that the boat was gone. Mind you, ships docked long enough to let off and board passengers. Missing the latter opportunity meant they wouldn't be back until daylight.

I can swim back, he decided and was about to remove a shoe when it dawned on him that the area was prone to shipwrecks. *On second thought, I'll wait it out*. He planted his butt in the sand and looked on wearily at the riffling waters coming ashore and crabs moving stealthily across the sand.

⁂

Not long after the lamplights died, a series of hollow bangs at the door roused them from slumber. Uri sprang up, heart thudding in his ear as he hurried to the door.

"Who is it?" he asked, resting his body against the door.

A weary, familiar voice resonated from the other end. He opened the door with more zest than necessary. "Don't you have anything better to do besides bothering us?"

"I do, but at the moment, I'm stranded."

Tabitha got out of bed, wrapped a shawl around her shift, and went to the door. She stared at Uri as he grumbled, moving off to the side and observed them while they spoke.

"What will you do?" Tabitha asked.

"I don't know. I don't have a lot of options."

She looked behind her, "We don't have an extra bed, but you're welcome to spend the night."

"I was hoping you'd say that. Thank you."
"You can sleep on Uri's bed and we'll share," she said authoritatively, looking at Uri sideways.

"Mom!"

"Son … a little consideration goes a long way. Besides, it's only for the night." Uri scowled.

"I hate to impose, but it's either this or I'll spend the night with the crabs on the beach as bedfellows."

"Come on son, let's get back to bed," his mother said and climbed into bed. Uri spent most of the night tossing and turning before he fell asleep, whereas Tabitha fell asleep in no time at all.

Shortly before sunrise, Detective Sloane's stirrings prompted Tabitha to sit up in bed.

"I didn't mean to wake you," he whispered.

"It's no bother at all; I'm usually up around this time. Would you like some tea?"

"Your offer is tempting, but I must get back to Vermouthshire," he said on the way out as he hurried down the road.

12

Sea waft washed over Detective Sloane as the ship coursed through the waves while he lounged on deck dogged down by thoughts of the case. Within an hour's time, Vermouthshire enlarged in the horizon and before long, the boat moored. After he got off the ship, Detective Sloane looked out to sea at the waves crashing against the vessels sailing away from the port, just long enough for him to forget his troubles. Then he walked to the station.

On the way in, he crossed paths with his superior just inside the entrance. "Have you made any progress with the case?"

"Nothing worth bragging about," Detective Sloane said.

Sergeant Eddie Pistone scratched the bald patch at the center of his head. "If you'd quit lollygagging, that'll change." That was far from the truth, but disproving Pistone's statement would do more harm than good. So he let it slide, knowing that he had three consecutive days off to cool his heels. Most of which he spent feeling sorry for himself, and for the remainder of the time, he lay in bed staring at the ceiling. By then, self-loathing had kicked in, so he ventured outdoors.

...

He could practically taste the brine in the air as the vessel sailed through the surf. After they docked in Draíocht Dol, Detective Sloane disembarked the boat carrying a bag and he sauntered down the boardwalk and over to the older man leaning against a wagon.

"Well, if it isn't the deserter. Thanks to you, I spent a night here."

"Sorry about that, but I told you, that place gives me the creeps. Besides, you couldn't pay me enough to go back there," Dudley tightened his lips, and exhaled.

Detective Sloane took out his wallet, removed paper money, and held it up. "I have a five dollar bill that says otherwise." Dudley appeared disinterested, so Detective Sloane increased his wager. "How about *ten* bucks?"

Dudley spun around and climbed the wagon. "Let's go."

"Not so fast—that's five dollars each way. You'll get the balance on the return trip," Detective Sloane said.

Dudley grimaced and let a breath out. "Come on, let's go."

In an hours' time, the carriage pulled into the O'Brien's yard. Sloane stepped down, walked over to the cabin, and knocked.

After a reasonable amount of time passed without a response, Dudley huffed. "Nobody's home. Let's go."

Detective Sloane glared at him. "Relax. We're not going anywhere until I say so." He rolled up his sleeves and walked out to the meadow. Standing midfield, he removed the *Birat Fertilizer* sack—a mixture of bird and bat excrement—from his bag and broke the seal. An egregious odor came from it, making his eyes water and causing an overwhelming urge to throw up. Despite the sickening feeling that had taken hold, Detective Sloane sprinkled the fertilizer and ambled down the line.

"What're you doing?" Uri who had entered the yard moments earlier yelled and jogged out to him. He was out of breath by the time he got to Detective Sloane. "Removing a tick is easier than getting rid of you!" He raged on and grabbed the sack out of Detective Sloane's hand.

"My apologies. I declared myself, but no one was home."

"What is this mess? Are you trying to sabotage us?" Uri asked, angrily.

"Why would I do that?" Detective Sloane's face bunched like a chastised pug.

"How the hell would I know?" He shoved the bag into Sloane's hand. "Leave."

Seeing Uri's temperament, Tabitha picked up the edge of her frock and hightailed it to where they were. "Uri please—" She held him by the forearm.

"Look—I'm not the enemy. I had some free time. I figured I'd help out … that's all."

"We don't need *your* help," Uri said begrudgingly.

Tabitha shot a fierce look at Uri, reminiscent of the way she looked at Anton before the wave hit. He backed away, trembling as if he were a rat cornered at the innards of a maze.

While he backed away, her gaze softened and returned to Detective Sloane. "That's quite admirable of you, but we don't accept handouts."

"If it makes you feel any better, you can offer me a home cooked meal. How does that sound?"

Tabitha looked appeased. "I suppose I could live with that."

With her blessing, he distributed what was left of the fertilizer and yanked weeds from the rows along the way. An hour into the task, Detective Sloane straightened his back, exhaled and looked in her direction the moment wisps of her hair flailed in the gentle wind. Tabitha wiped sweat from her brow and turned to him, "Are you ready to call it quits?"

"Yes. It's too hot."

"Then, it's time to get out of the kitchen," she said and then laughed. A smile, albeit rare, showed on his face.

13

Since he was last there, the harvests had grown to knee-length—quite different from the state they were in before. Detective Sloane stood at the center of the field admiring his handy work. Tabitha came up from behind and stood beside him, "They're coming along nicely, aren't they?"

"Yes, they are. It's getting late and I should be on my way." As he put a foot forth to walk away, Tabitha held onto his forearm. An uneasy feeling surfaced inside him as he turned to her.

"You should stay for supper."

His face brightened, "Yes, I should."

The cabin livened as they gathered around the table, speaking of the mishaps they encountered during the day. Even Uri's mood lightened—something Tabitha hadn't seen much of since they left their homeland. Eventually, as the food lessened, their conversation dwindled. After which Detective Sloane eyed her tenderly, "You're a great cook. A man could easily die portly here," he chortled and stood. "It was so good, I'll wash the dishes."

Tabitha blushed, "Thank you, but that's not necessary."

"I must insist." He gathered the dishes and hustled to the kitchen before she could talk him out of it.

14

Vigorous pounding drew their attention to the front door, each strike more powerful than the last. At that hour in the evening, she wasn't expecting anyone, but by the temperament of the knock, she knew she'd kept the person waiting for far too long. Tabitha left the kitchen and went over to the door.

"Who is it?" she asked and shortly after heard a faintly groaned response.

"Who's—?" This time, she heard a brassier moan. Tabitha looked at Uri, both filled with curious unease.

Uri joined her. "Quit horsing around," he yelled, "Who is it?"

Uri heard something but it was indistinguishable, so he opened the door. At that instant, a disgusting, off-putting rank odor crept up his nose, corrupting his senses. Just outside the threshold, an emaciated, cerulean-eyed man donning a crown of twigs atop his matted hair and tattered clothing, whimpered. Uri couldn't help but stare at the man's exposed chest, *two–four–six*—counting off his ribs, and cringed—*dear God*. He looked on in disbelief as the man reached, but failed to grasp him and instead, crumpled to the floor.

Horrified, she backed into the table slack-jawed, and blindly pulled the chair out from behind. Tabitha plopped down listlessly, her life force drained, and then started to return in second-by-second intervals. In her eyes, the room spun like a top, gradually losing power as cold sweat induced an all-encompassing quiver.

Detective Sloane rushed to her side as Tabitha continued to stare at the man slumped on the floor. At a loss for words, Uri couldn't bear to lower his eyes to him.

"Tabitha," Detective Sloane said and gently shook her but got no response.

"Tabitha, I'm home," the disheveled man uttered and he reached out to her.

"Marc—" she said his name and yet it sounded surreal.

Uri lowered his gaze as she said Marc's name and then she went limp and slipped from the chair into Detective Sloane's arms.

15

Detective Sloane helped Uri carry Marc to the bed and sat him down. Free from their grasp, Marc slumped down on the mattress like a sack of wheat and let out a yawning wheeze.

"I should leave." Detective Sloane backed away toward the door, turned and looked outside. "When his health improves, I'd like to have a word with him." No one looked in his direction or bothered to reply.

Long after Sloane departed, Uri sat at the dining table gazing at Marc as he lay in bed shivering with the covers pulled up to his neck. Tabitha sat at his bedside and placed a cool rag on his forehead.

"We looked everywhere for you, Marc. Where were you?"

His response—incoherent, delirious babble—rang out. Each time she touched his warm flesh, strangely it ignited a lingering chill. Thus far, she'd rid him of the pungent odor, and tried to nurse him back to health but her efforts did little to break his fever.

Seeing her husband in such a fragile state brought tears to her eyes. "Where were you?" she asked again but Marc just stared past her as if she wasn't there.

***

In the hopes of improving his condition, they reached out to Dr. Randall who was a man well into his mid-forties. His looks defied his age, not to mention his small stature. He took Marc's vitals as he sat at the edge of the bed. After detaching the stethoscope from his ear, Dr. Randall looked at Tabitha.

"I'm afraid there's not much else I can do—at least nothing that would change the outcome. What I can do is provide pain medication to keep him comfortable. I wish I could do more." He took a bottle of pills from his medical bag and gave it to her.

An admission that numbed her, Tabitha wept as she held the bottle loosely. "No-no, he won't die. He just returned home!" Tabitha hollered through an eruption of strained cries and slumped to her knees.

Uri knelt beside her and held her in his arms.

67

"No!" Tabitha wailed, freeing herself from his embrace and thumped his back.

"I'm truly sorry, Mrs. O'Brien," Dr. Randall's lips quivered as he spoke. He pulled a flask from his inner coat pocket, took a swig and tucked it back in his jacket, patted his temple with a hankie, and left the cabin.

16

Tabitha held a bedside vigil as Marc lay there unresponsive. It was the least she could do, especially after she'd accepted his death so easily without the benefit of a body for confirmation. Mourning her son Jon was a feat by itself, and now she was on the verge of losing her husband a second time.

"If I weren't so hell-bent on revenge, you'd be in good health. It wouldn't change what happened to our boy, but at least we'd have each other. I'm sorry." She closed her eyes and wept silently. "If I'd known what I was capable of, I wouldn't have unleashed my wrath; then again, I had no way of knowing beforehand the damage I'd cause."

By then, it was too late for 'what ifs,' no way to undo the damage that was already done, let alone lessen their pain. Her attempts to feed him solid food and fluids were unsuccessful and with each passing day, a sickly odor surfaced that lingered as his condition continued to worsen.

Given those circumstances, they took turns tending to him, and during those times, neither of them got much sleep. Five days after his return, Tabitha sat Uri down and held his hand.

"It's time," she said, holding back tears, "we should say goodbye before it's too late. He won't be with us for much longer," she concluded and then broke down.

"I can't. I barely said hello … I'm not ready to say goodbye." Uri squeezed her hand and wept.

•••

Whether they liked it or not, later that evening they said their goodbyes and spent the rest of the night fighting the urge to sleep. Eventually, they fell asleep and before long morning came. At sunrise, they woke to guttural sounds that prompted them to look anxiously about. Tabitha walked over to Marc, cast the sheet aside, and stared at him in disbelief as he shifted restlessly. A welcomed sight, especially after they'd suffered through the last few days, seeing him barely clinging to life and saying their heartfelt farewells.

"That's the spirit. Don't give up. Fight it." Once she said that, his limbs relaxed and his eyes opened slightly. After which his head quickly jerked to the side. Seconds later a tar-like substance spewed from his mouth and hung like melted mozzarella, then detached and splattered on the floor.

17

All of her efforts to converse with Marc were futile except for the gestured response and off-putting moans. His failure to communicate compounded her distress as she sat sulking in the dark room illuminated by candlelight, observing him while she contemplated her next move. Tabitha moved to the edge of her seat. After a closer look, she realized that he was asleep, but vocal.

It's common, she reminded herself. *People talk in their sleep all the time*. Yet, his conversation was lengthy, poignant somehow. So much so that even in the REM stage—active sleep—he opened his eyes, flung the covers aside and got out of bed. His stony glance widened as he looked directly at her and yet it was as if she wasn't there. Tabitha stood and stepped aside, allowing him to walk past her.

"Where are you going?" He kept walking toward the door. "How much longer will you keep me in the dark? Don't you think I deserve to know?" She sighed heavily, her glare reminiscent to daggers in his back as he went out the door. "I'm your wife," she raised her voice.

Abruptly, he turned to her, "It didn't look that way when I returned home and saw another man in our kitchen."

Tabitha's mouth fell open. He turned his back to her and walked away. She waited until he was out of sight, and then followed him out to the field. Tabitha observed as Marc gathered twigs, set them down in a pile and roughly started a fire. After the fire was lit, he glared at it, tightened his fists, tilted his head back and belted out a roar in an octave that paled any beast's howl that she'd ever heard. At that instant, the flames leapt well above his head. Tabitha trembled while processing the troubling sight as the air filled with the reek of seared flesh. By that time, the heightened flames emphasized a side of his face that had turned to molten flesh–copiously hanging from the facial musculature attached to his skull, eclipsed only by a cantankerous, lipless grin and partially exposed teeth smeared with blood.

She blinked and took a fresh look at the unfolding spectacle. This time, his face showed no sign of wasting or an exposed skull, and yet she couldn't stop trembling. Not even the obscurity of the night could hide the effect his peculiar behavior had on her. She closed her eyes and made herself small behind the tree, but moments later dared to peek just as Marc dropped to his knees and let out a quivering cry. After he was through, he trekked home calmly as if nothing had ever happened.

Understandably shaken, Tabitha stayed out there for a while but once she came to her senses, she went back to the cabin.

"Good morning," she said, greeting them as she entered the doorway.

Uri responded in kind from where he and Marc sat tableside drinking tea, but Marc did not attempt to acknowledge her. It pained Uri; this wasn't what they were like before the flood. Back then, they were nothing but loving toward each other. Uri gulped as an uncomfortable silence filled the room. Thus far, he'd managed to evade their tense exchanges by feigning sleep. On other occasions, he tried as best he could to be invisible until their tiffs blew over, but this time, there was no escaping them, he was caught between wolves and there was no telling when their marital strife would end.

18

"Give us the room ... I'd like to speak with your father."

Uri left the cabin and sat beneath the tree at the side of the house.

"I've wronged you—of this I'm certain, but I've been true to you even in death," she said from a distance. "He's been—"

"I know what he's been doing—sniffing around you like a hound in heat, and you, my dear wife, beamed in his presence; praised him as if he were a deity," he said as disdain filled his eyes. "It made me sick to my stomach."

Tabitha lowered her gaze. Then, a thought came to mind, "Wait a minute—were you spying on us?" she asked, lips tensing as she exhaled softly. "I've loved you for as long as I can remember." She widened the space between them. "I love *you,* Marc. You're the *only* man I've *ever* loved," she said as an involuntary twitch briefly jerked her. Tabitha turned from him and wept. He stepped forward, turned her, and lifted her chin until their eyes met. "I don't want him around here, or circling you. After all, you're *my* wife. Am I being clear?"

"Very, but he'll be back, no matter what you or I say."

"What for?" he asked, tensing his jaw.

Tabitha widened the gap between them. "He wants to talk to you about Donovan Kingsley's disappearance."

Marc sucked his teeth. "Disappearance? I don't know where he is."

"I know, but he'll ask anyway. Actually ..." she folded her arms, "... I have a few questions for you too, so he can wait in line."

"You do, huh?" Marc raised a brow.

"Of course I do. I've been inquiring ever since you came home. Where were you?"

"Did it ever occur to you that you didn't look hard enough?" he went off topic.

Stunned by his reproach, Tabitha stared at him but said nothing. His nostrils flared as he exhaled, "I was unconscious and woke with a splitting headache. At first, I was disoriented, but it didn't take long to realize that I wasn't on Draíocht Dol. In fact, I was marooned on a spit of land east of the coast," he said and then laughed it off.

"Why didn't you signal for help?"

"I was injured, barely able to move, lying out in the open, baking day in, day out, feeling the brunt of the sun. With that said, I couldn't signal even if I wanted to. Outside of the critters, I was the only human being on that God forsaken island."

"If that's the case, how did you get back to Draíocht Dol?" she asked, slightly confused.

"I'm not sure." His temple wrinkled. "I was near the end of life—dehydrated, starving, and in a state of perpetual delirium." A daydreamer's gaze came over him. "Some say light ushers us to the other side, but I'd say otherwise."

Mentally, he returned to the moment where a realm of duplicating rays of light beheld him, where a cloaked man spoke to him. About what? He couldn't say—even if he knew.

"I recall saying, 'I'd do anything to return to my family', and closed my eyes. When I awoke the following day, I was on the coast of Draíocht Dol." His admission struck her as peculiar in nature, but at least he had confided in her.

"All that matters is that you made it home." She held him tenderly while she tried to make sense of what he'd said.

19

As was tradition, the O'Briens reaped the yields and stocked the wagon. Marc helped when he could, and at other times, sat beneath a tree, bearing witness to their toils. His eyes softened as they followed her while she moved toward him.

"Are you coming? I won't take no for an answer." Tabitha helped him to his feet and into her embrace, an act he repaid with a kiss on the cheek.

As he neared them, Uri cleared his throat, "We should go."

Tabitha blushed, revealing a demure smile. She held Marc's hand and led the way with Uri trailing them to the cabin. They'd been that way lately—affectionate—every moment they had to themselves, he'd unsuspectingly interrupt an intimate exchange between them. A grand achievement when he considered that not long ago they were at each other's throats. Consequently, their tender interaction made him reminisce about the lovely nurse he'd met at St.

Vincent's Hospital. He hoped they'd meet again. A thought that made a surreal smile spread on his face.

He mounted the wagon and drove out to the coast with his parents at his side. Along the way, Marc took in the setting and reminisced about the time when they'd first came to Draíocht Dol and had rode out to the countryside to where the illusory beauty of their homestead caught his eyes.

His attention shifted to her. "You're a strong woman who has accomplished a lot in my absence," his voice cracked with emotion.

"One never knows how capable they are until they're tested. It's a good thing we're no strangers to struggle. The desire to survive is of the utmost importance—and at times a strange bedfellow, but a motivational one," Tabitha sighed. "Then again, it keeps you going—even when death would be kinder." Saddened, she held him close.

Moments later, Uri parked adjacent to the shop and tied the horses to the rail. Released from her grasp, Marc turned to step down from his perch and came around to help her down. At that moment, he beheld the black of her eyes turning white. Her head wagged incongruously, blurring until it appeared as many heads instead of one. Milliseconds later, she went limp; her wrists bent inward and saliva dripped from her chin. Uri stood aside, immovable, mouth ajar. All while, unnerving thoughts surfaced in his head pertaining to the how, why, and what made such a feat possible.

Witnessing her coming apart before his very eyes, Marc reached for her only to draw back his hand as a faint mist eerily seeped from her eyes, permitting fragments of images from nights past to come into frame, images of Marc's partially exposed skull, and moist facial musculature draped with partially limp flesh replayed in rapid successions. Even as all of this was taking place, she fervently writhed to free the images from sight. Blood—lots of it—draped the left side of his chin and slipped down the ruined side of his face like the sap of a tree. Meanwhile, everything around her reeked of death.

Five minutes passed before her burden alleviated and then she was freed from her visions. Tabitha fell forward and then sideways off the edge of the seat. Marc caught her and breathed a sigh of relief.

"Are you okay?" he asked, holding her close.

"I think so," she wiped cold sweat from her temple. "It's nothing, really," she replied, making light of the incident.

Whereas Uri trembled as he stood on the sidelines quietly observing while Marc carried her to the store and sat Tabitha down in a chair out front. As Uri approached the stairs, Marc held his forearm. His clammy hands made Uri shiver. "Keep a close eye on your mother," he said loud enough that only Uri could hear.

Uri nodded and descended the steps. "I'll bring the produce inside." Marc returned to her.

"Don't make a fuss on my account." She swayed a hand dismissively, got up and trudged down the stairs. Marc sighed and sat in the seat she previously occupied.

"I'll take care of it," Uri reiterated in a slightly agitated tone.

Tabitha spun around, climbed the steps, and sat on a seat across from her husband. After their debate, Uri cleared the wagon bed, put the crops on display, and stood at the entrance, looking beyond the shoreline where a sail stuck out in the distance. In no time, the ship docked and passengers exited like chattel. Most were shopkeepers from Vermouthshire looking for a bargain, and the rest were folks returning home.

Detective Sloane wove his way through the crowd to the storefront and greeted them accordingly. "Good day, Mr. and Mrs. O'Brien."

At once, Marc thoroughly eyed the strapping man before him as a grim look spread on Tabitha's face. Even as she secretly hoped that her husband would be civil towards him. "Forgive me, but your name is evading me at the moment," Marc said even though he knew the detective's name.

"It's Detective Sloane."

"Yes, that's right. We have fresh produce for sale."

"That's good to know, but it's not why I'm here. I'd like to speak with you about Donovan Kingsley."

Marc grabbed an apple from the crate and peeled it while he spoke, "I don't know much about him, but I'll tell you what I know."

"I'd appreciate that."

"Would you like some?" Marc asked, temporarily distracting him.

"No, thank you."

Uri came out front. "You again," he said and Tabitha palmed her forehead.

"I'll be gone before you know it."

"That would be nice. The last thing we need is you scaring off potential customers after all our efforts."

"Uri, I'll handle this. Carry on," Marc said, sternly sending Uri back inside.

"Where was I?" Detective Sloane looked down at the pad. "Ah, yes. Did you have a working relationship with Mr. Kingsley?"

"I can't say that I did. He was interested in purchasing my harvest, but with the stipulation that I couldn't sell my crops anywhere else. Only a fool would take him up on his offer, but not me," Marc said with disdain. "Most people dream of becoming wealthy, but what I find most interesting is the process of making something out of nothing. For instance, at the start of the growing season, farmers get their hand's dirty planting seeds, but by the end of it, they can reap the fruits of their labor. They eat what they can and sell the rest, and if they're business-minded, they get to pass the business down to their sons and they to their sons. If I'd sold out to Donovan Kingsley it would be the equivalent of giving up on that dream."

Detective Sloane nodded. "I see." Clearly, Marc was a principled man.

"Mr. Kingsley wasn't thrilled with my decision, but what's mine is mine and what's his is his. You can appreciate that, can't you?"

"I can," Detective Sloane replied apprehensively.

"I've worked hard for what I have and I'll be damned if I let someone who's never endured a day of hard work in his life cheat me out of my livelihood, let alone my family. They're my most prized possessions … do you get my drift?"

Halfway through Marc's lengthy response, Detective Sloane began to wonder if they were still discussing his connection to Donovan Kingsley. He gulped. "I believe I do, Mr. O'Brien."

"Well … if that's all, I'd like to get back to selling our goods."

"Yes, of course. Thank you for your time."

Leaving the vicinity, Detective Sloane couldn't help but feel gutted like a fish, only to have his entrails—*hopes*—tossed aside. He tucked the notepad in his pocket, walked back to the pier, and boarded the ship. Not long after he boarded the vessel, the ship set sail for Vermouthshire.

During the journey, Detective Sloane sat below the sails with a deepening sadness in his eyes. Unlike the previous trips, this journey forced him to look within himself to determine where his focus should lie at this point in the case. After much consideration, he peered out at the vast deep with the wind sweeping through his hair and hesitantly buried his misplaced desire for Tabitha O'Brien there.

20

At day's end, Marc calculated their profits, set-aside money, and put the rest in the cash box. Moments later, he walked over to where Tabitha was wiping down the counter on the other side of the store.

"I'd like you to go to Vermouthshire and buy something for yourself, and while you're at it, pick up something for Uri," he placed the balance of the money in her hand and locked it in her grasp.

Tabitha smiled at him and said, "As you wish."

The following day, she got dressed for the trip to Vermouthshire and stood in front of the mirror. Uri came up behind her as she tended to her face. "You look beautiful, as always, Mother."

"You're too kind. You'll make some woman a fine husband someday." Tabitha softened as she observed his smile that reached his ears. "I'm planning on purchasing a few items for myself and for you as well. Would you like to come? That is if your father doesn't need you."

"I'll find out." Uri jogged out to the field where Marc was planting seeds. "Father," he yelled, approaching him. "Do you need my help with anything?" he asked, almost out of breath.

"I might. Why?"

"Well," Uri moved his hair out of his face. "Mom suggested that I go to Vermouthshire with her."

"Save yourself a headache. You'll be more comfortable here," he said and chuckled.

"Oh, I don't mind," Uri insisted.

Marc looked up at him. This was a first—Uri having the slightest interest in going shopping with his mother. "All right, son what is it?"

Blushing, Uri responded enthusiastically, "There's this girl, Samantha. I like—"

"Hope she's worth the trouble." An amused smile graced Marc's face.

"Besides after what happened the other day at the shop, it's best that she is not left alone."

"Yes, I suppose you're right … go on. I can manage without you." Thrilled, Uri hurried back to the cabin. "Good Luck," Marc hollered in his direction.

Looking back briefly, Uri smiled and then jogged the rest of the way. Shortly afterward, they rode out to the pier and boarded the next boat to Vermouthshire.

•••

Marc labored out in the fields, planting seeds with a newfound energy that allowed him to work, a grand accomplishment considering his previous state. It wasn't that long ago since he'd returned broken and near death. Living in the presence of his family was more than he could ask for, in fact, he had … when he thought the end was near.

Thankfully, since that time, relations with his wife improved. How could it not? She fattened him with care and the bond between him and Uri strengthened with each passing day. Yet, he felt disgusted with himself for not easing their pain when he'd first returned. Instead, he had watched them toil as they mourned him. A decent husband, or human being for that matter, would've put ill feelings aside and returned home, but not him. Instead of going home, Marc had camped out, observing them from afar, nurturing unhealthy notions.

Trying to push the thoughts aside, he straightened his back, wiped sweat from his temple with the sleeve of his shirt and sighed. His castaway experience paled in comparison to the difficulties they faced. Looking around, he couldn't deny the strides they had made. Shamefaced, he squatted down at the base of a tree, eyes moistening as he rested his head on bent knees.

To their credit, when they first came to Astonia, they held no illusions of the transition being stress-free, and yet it turned out to be much worse than they imagined.

The life of a settler isn't easy. Anyone who thought otherwise would be fooling themselves. Settlers set out for uncharted territories, lay claim to the land, and build homes from the ground up, he thought. They'd accomplished that and yet Marc groaned. *Rich folk like Donovan Kingsley know nothing about such matters; they specialize in acquisitions after the difficult work is done.* Whether he liked it or not, experiencing hardship taught them to be resilient.

21

Vacationers and natives alike navigated the shopping district. The O'Briens were among them; they entered shops, tried on articles of clothing, and when they didn't quite fit, had them tailored to their specifications.

After they accomplished their main goal, Uri turned to his mother. "There's someone I'd like to find. It won't take long."

"When you're through, meet me at the eatery. It's next to the haberdashery."

"I know the place. I'll meet you there," he said and parted ways.

On the way to the hospital, he came across a flower shop but didn't think to stop at first. Somewhere down the line, he doubled back, bought a bouquet of flowers, and hastened his steps. Uri looked at the time and recalled that her shift would be over soon and hustled onward. By the time he arrived at St. Vincent's Hospital, the shifts had already changed. Only a few stragglers exiting the building remained. Uri peered at the flowers in hand and sighed as he fretted over his timing.

"Are you waiting for someone?" A raspy voice came from the side of the building.

He looked over his shoulder and saw an older woman smoking in a corner.

"Yes, Samantha. I don't remember her last name, but she's about this tall," he estimated her height by hand, "blonde hair, and full, blue eyes."

"I know her. She left not long before you arrived."

"Which way did she go?"

"That way," she pointed.

"Thank you, Ma'am," he said and then he ran off in that direction.

.•.

Half a mile away, Tabitha traveled down the block with their purchases in hand, admiring the window dressings of the shops flanked by Royal Poinciana trees. Their flaccid dark brown pods made a shrill sound, fueled by the slightest breeze. As she walked the path, striped flowers wafted downward and once they were at head-level, the segments appeared akin to a rose. Partly amused, but otherwise curious, she proceeded on the regal path of petals at her feet that turned black as her shoes made contact with them and as she raised her feet, they developed into a gooey, tar-like substance that adhered like gum to the sole of her shoes.

At that point, a legion of hands—gray, pallid ones—emerged from the goo and began to grapple at her feet, ulcerous from decay, and inundated with pus-filled boils that ruptured, releasing a pungent chloroform odor. The perplexing sight drained the color from her face, after which the legion of hands held onto her ankles and pulled. Before she knew it, her ankles became one with the sidewalk.

A woman exiting one of the stores approached her, noticing how visibly shaken Tabitha was. "Are you okay, Ma'am?" she asked and placed a hand on Tabitha's shoulder. Only then was she freed.

Tabitha gasped for breath as if she'd been underwater for far too long, and at any minute would draw her last breath. "I'm fine, thank you." The Good Samaritan hesitated and then walked away. Shortly after, the woman spun around and looked back at Mrs. O'Brien before continuing on her way.

For a fleeting moment, Tabitha closed her eyes and tried to think of anything—*anything* other than what she experienced minutes earlier. However, even during her efforts to do so, the image resurfaced. Trembling, Tabitha opened her eyes and looked down at her feet. Contrary to what she'd seen before, spotted vermilion-colored segments, not black rose petals, blanketed the sidewalk.

From then on, everything blurred and then cleared. By then, Tabitha had arrived at her destination - the eatery - but had no recollection of how she got there. She took in a deep breath and exhaled, and then entered the establishment. The host greeted her upon entry, escorted her to a table by the window and took her order.

❦❦❦

Inundated with sweat and short-winded, Uri gauged his odds of finding Samantha before they left, and decided to end his search. He dragged his foot as he went along the sidewalk until an object in a window display gave him pause. Uri stood there, watching skewered horses adorned with painted saddles and gold flourishes encased in a cake-sized merry-go-round circulate, entrancing him with its whimsical presentation.

"It's beautiful, isn't it?" a woman asked in a mature raspy voice.

"It is," he replied without vigor, and continued to look at the merry-go-round.

"I come here after work sometimes and stare at it for hours. It helps me forget whatever went wrong that day," she went on while he sighed with disinterest.

"Men are hard to read. I use to care for a man, but he's unavailable ninety-nine percent of the time. It pains me because I was quite fond of him," she said and he felt the urge to look her way. There in the flesh beside him stood Samantha with flushed cheeks, and a red nose, speaking in a tenor coarse enough to grate cheese.

"I went to the hospital to look for you."

"I left early. I think I'm coming down with something."

Uri's lips tightened as he looked down at the wilting flowers. Then he gave them to her. "These are for you. I hope you feel better."

Samantha brought the flowers up to her nose and smelled them. "Thank you."

"I'm sorry for not staying in touch, but I've been preoccupied with rebuilding our family's home and business—"

"I'm not cross with you. I was only trying to get your attention earlier," she said with an ephemeral smile.

He smiled and nodded. "Thanks for understanding, but shouldn't you be on your way home seeing that you're not feeling well?"

"Yes, but first I must purchase some medicine at the apothecary."

"If it's okay with you, I'd like to buy it for you." He took her hand, placed it on his forearm, and walked with her to the location. "I don't have much to offer, but my heart is yours … if you want it. We can go at whatever pace you like."

"I'm not in the business of accepting vital organs or medicine from strange men, *but* I'll make an exception," she said and chuckled.

Uri blushed as he muffled his laughter. "I wish I could spend more time with you, but I'm meeting my mother at the eatery." They entered the apothecary, and with her blessing, he paid for her the treatment. Shortly after that, they left the store and strode outdoors.

Outside the storefront, he faced her as he held both of her hands and looked her in the eye. "Take care of yourself. I'll try to come back in a week to check up on you," Uri kissed her hand.

"If you can't, I'll understand," Samantha muttered, and rested her head on his chest.

They parted ways but Samantha stood there for a while watching him walk halfway down the block before she left.

Tabitha drank a cup of tea and looked out the window the moment Uri passed before entering. She waved to get his attention. Uri joined her and ordered a cup of tea.

"How did it go?" she asked and put the cup to her lips.

"It went well. You'd like Samantha. I know I do," he beamed. "She's the girl you saw the last time."

Tabitha's eyes lit up when she smiled—an achievement considering what she had gone through earlier. "And the boy became a man." Her smile dwindled some. "Falling in love will do that."

"It'll be dark soon. We should go." Tabitha signaled for the check, paid, and they left the establishment. "When will you introduce her to the family?" she asked as they walked side-by-side back to the pier.

"It's too soon. I don't want to scare her off."

Tabitha smiled, as she looked at him sideways and put her hand on his forearm. Their slow stroll down the pathways garnered coy greetings of acknowledgment—the norm, even for strangers walking about town. In passing, they came across a fair-haired woman holding a baby with ringlets bordering her slender face. The child, now at an age where she could sit on her mother's hip, waved at the couple and smiled, revealing a single tooth. Tabitha smiled and waved at her. Instinctively, the mother smiled as well while the O'Briens continued down the walkway.

A few feet down the road, the child's mother stopped abruptly. *They look familiar, but from where?* In the spur of the moment, it dawned on her where she had seen them, although this time they were unsoiled and looked no different from anyone else. That's what threw her off at first.

On that fateful day when she had first seen them, Tabitha and Uri had hastily crossed paths with her as they navigated the shopping district with soft tissue coating their faces and clothing discolored with blood. Their appearance had made them stick out like vagrants in a park. After deriving a conclusion, Lenna Matheson's eyes turned feral. She held her baby to her bosom and ran swiftly to the police station while the little one wailed.

22

By the time she arrived at the police station, sweat saturated most of Lenna's dress as well as her daughter Cristina's hair. After exhaling sharply, she entered the police station winded and approached the high counter. "Is Detective Sloane in?"

Inside the relatively quiet wood paneled room, only one out of four officers there looked up when she spoke. "He left a while ago," he said from the corner of the room. "Is there something I can help you with?" he asked while walking over to her.

"I need to speak with him. I have some information that I'd like to share with—" The beginnings of a muted cry came from the child. Out of habit, Lenna began to bounce Cristina lightly on her hip.

"I can take your information. He'll get back to you at his earliest convenience."

She gave him her name and number and exited the precinct. Halfway down the street, Lenna saw

Detective Sloane leaving a coffee shop and called out to him. Upon noticing her, he jogged over to where she was.

"The couple," she anxiously blurted out. "They're downtown as we speak."

Sloane poured out the rest of his coffee. "Come with me." Lenna and child got in his patrol car and they drove to the shopping district a mile away.

"Where did you see them?" he asked briefly, taking his eye off the road as he looked at her.

"They were headed toward Dorcas' Haberdashery."

But as they cruised through town, Lenna saw no sign of them. Detective Sloane parked in a vacant spot a few stores ahead. He stood in the middle of the block with his hands rested on his hips and visually canvassed the area. *Where are they?*

Seeing how disappointed he was, Lenna tried to reassure him. "I ran to the station the moment I realized who they were, but apparently I wasn't fast enough," she said and leaned against the car. "I can't imagine where they could've gone in such a short time, other than returning home," Lenna said without giving it much thought, but her comment spurred him to act.

"Let's go," Detective Sloane said anxiously and got in the car.

They pulled out of the lot moments later with the siren blaring and came to a screeching stop on the part of the dock cordoned off by thick blocks of wood and ship rope. The car doors flew open, Detective Sloane and his occupants came out and hustled down to the mooring area where a boat launched no more than five minutes earlier. With little time to spare, Lenna's line of sight filtered through the passengers on deck.

"There. That's them," her heart raced as she eagerly jabbed the air pointing them out.

Now that he'd had visual confirmation, Detective Sloane's jaw slackened. There they were, Tabitha and Uri O'Brien standing at the side of the boat, gazing out to sea. Unfortunately, the boat in question was too far to stop them from leaving. He looked on helplessly as they sailed away and got smaller in the distance.

"It's the last one," he said and turned toward her. "When the ship returns, it'll be moored until morning, so there's no reason why we should stay here. I'll take you home."

After Detective Sloane took Lenna and Cristina home, he returned to the station, traveled down the hall, and stood outside Pistone's door. He stood there for a while before he knocked. Shortly after, he entered and spent the next fifteen minutes bringing Sergeant Pistone up to speed on his findings.

"What do you mean they got away?" Pistone raised his voice, "Why didn't you stop the boat from leaving?"

That would be impossible unless I turned into Poseidon and pulled the boat back to the dock, he thought but didn't dare to say it. "The boat had already left the dock, sir."

Sergeant Pistone grimaced. "Jesus wept. This case has about the same pace as molasses moving downhill. Wrap this case up with a bow so we can put it to bed, Detective Sloane." Sergeant Pistone scratched the bald patch at the top of his head.

"Yes, sir."

Baffled by Detective Sloane's futile attempts to link the O'Briens to Donovan Kingsley's disappearance, Sergeant Pistone let out an exasperated breath. "Interview them first thing tomorrow—you hear me? And while you're at it, *lay off* the charm. The nice cop act has gotten you nowhere. It's bad cop time. Can you do that?" he spoke loud enough for their conversation to penetrate the room.

"Yes—sir," he stammered, but this time in rote mode.

"All right," Pistone extended his hammy hand, "leave." Detective Sloane closed the door behind him and let out a deep sigh.

As Detective Sloane emerged from the corridor, Detective Kershaw smirked as he passed him on his way to the filing cabinets. When Sloane reached the center of the room, the other officers began to drum on their desks. Dutch's voice eclipsed the musical compilation, "Detective Sloane, the strongest man within a 50-mile radius, and the *only* man capable of hauling a massive boat back to shore with his bare hands," Detective Dutch Kershaw joked.

The room erupted with short-lived cackles. Word got around fast in the station; it always did, especially when daddy dearest – better known as Sergeant Eddie Pistone - dropped the gavel on someone. Just about all of them had been there, but today it was his turn. Detective Sloane forced a smile and strode to his desk.

♪♪♪

While his wife and son finished shopping in downtown Vermouthshire, Marc planted the last of his seeds and freshened up. Afterward, he stood before the mirror, applying shaving soap to his lengthy beard, and removed the hair using a straight razor. With each swipe, lines of hair fell to the ground, and in no time, he was clean-shaven. He continued the trend by cutting his hair, and then rubbed a dab of petroleum jelly on his hands and slicked his hair back.

After hearing the familiar sound of the horses entering the yard, Marc ventured outside. Upon sight of him, Tabitha's eyes widened and a smile spread across her face. Marc met them at the wagon and lent her his hand as she stepped down.

"I thought you'd never cut that thing," she said beaming and then kissed him.

"I was long overdue for a shave."

"You look scrumptious." She hooked her arm in his and they went inside. Uri grabbed the shopping bags and entered the house behind them.

Marc turned to him and asked, "How did it go?"

"It went better than I expected."

"That's my boy." Marc patted Uri on the back.

23

Unexpectedly, overnight a nor'easter developed 30 miles offshore, and by landfall, Aerona and Draíocht Dol were battered with ten-foot barbaric waves. Meanwhile, the howls of gale-force gusts kept most residents, including the O'Briens, up for most of the night, hunkered down inside their cabins. Draíocht Dol, still mending from its last bout with nature felt the brunt of the wind-driven rain saturating the area, weighing down trees and everything else.

Soon, overwash opened the seawall and channeled small rivers of salt water through the roads and pathways, which eventually threatened seaport businesses and residential properties inland. Though ravaged by nature, the shops held up relatively well compared to the total loss they experienced the last time and instead escaped with minor damages.

Eventually, the nor'easter's reach expanded to Vermouthshire where powerful waves battered the shopping district, uprooting trees and shattering windows. The nor'easter's heavy rain pounded rooftops, poured onto walkways and streets alike, flooding them, raising water levels to dangerous heights. Given no warning, boat owners didn't have the opportunity to store their vessels elsewhere. To make matters worse, a boat moored at the dock broke free, washed ashore, and landed in the center of the road near the shops closest to the entrance of the dock.

Whether it was a blessing or a curse—Detective Sloane couldn't say, but the present weather conditions didn't allow him, let alone anyone else, to leave. He reported the conditions of the downtown area to Sergeant Pistone, who wasn't thrilled to hear it, but this time he realized there wasn't anything Detective Sloane could do about it.

While the weather continued to worsen on Vermouthshire, the wind died down and conditions gradually improved on Draíocht Dol. Later that afternoon, Marc cracked the front door. What wind remained pushed the door, but he braced himself and held it in place. From what he could see, for every few feet, small rivers fed a larger one near the entrance. More trees than he could count had been weakened during the downpour and leaned at all angles throughout the property. Other than that, the condition of their cash crops was still a mystery. Estimating the true damage was all but impossible with the location of the field at the furthest end of the property. Marc sighed and closed the door.

"How bad is it?" Tabitha asked from the kitchen.

"It's unclear at this point. We'll know more once we get out there."

At nightfall, they ate dinner and afterward formulated a plan to clear the land while Tabitha cleared the table. It was then that a heavy thud, followed by a dragging scratch on the front door grabbed their attention, trailed off and then it happened again.

"Who is it?" Uri asked, but no one responded.

24

Eight hours earlier

Even a fellow officer who had yet to make detective, Calvin Brinker, who'd been on the force a year prior to Detective Kershaw and Detective Sloane, had his say.

"Sloane doesn't know when to call it quits. I suppose you could consider his persistence an asset in this line of work, but men like him end up beating dead horses until they turn zombie and gallop away."

DK laughed hysterically. "You should know; after all, you're the master of spewing absurdities. You should try applying for a job at the 'Town & Country Bulletin'," an up, and coming ragtag publication that circulated once a month. The other officers laughed at his expense.

"Who knows? You might move on to bigger and better things." Kershaw placed a file on his desk, retrieved his coat from the rack, and walked to the exit.

Without realizing it, he passed Detective Sloane out front. He'd gotten soaked while he was at the waterfront area getting an update on the status of the boat service to report to Sergeant Pistone, and at present was drying off at the entrance of the station. Detective Sloane's back rested against the clay bricks which was where he observed Kershaw running out into the rain with his coat overhead and entering a Model-T police vehicle. Kershaw hadn't noticed him in passing, but once he got in, he saw Detective Sloane standing outside.

Unbeknownst to them, Detective Sloane was at the entrance, close enough to hear everything they'd said and smacked his lips. *First* cometh *praises, then criticism*. As puerile as his comrades were, they served a greater purpose—the people of Vermouthshire. After some time passed, he entered the station dry enough to have a sit down with Sergeant Pistone.

Hours later, Samantha trundled into the station, partially wet with her hands and knees bruised, and walked over to the counter. "I'd like to file a report."

Recuperating from the 'bash Detective Sloane' debacle, coupled with a tense meeting with the Sergeant, Detective Sloane shuffled through a pile of paperwork on his desk. All but one of his turncoat coworkers had left for the day, and by the looks of it, he was on his way out as well. Looking up briefly, Sloane noticed a disheveled, yet attractive woman standing in the intake area.

With merely three desks between him and the intake counter, he often heard the details of every case, especially the big ones, and often times the '*snacks*' as the officers called them. And by the looks of it, it was snack time.

"I'm on my way out," Officer Pierson said, "but—" he glanced over his shoulder, "—Sloane, I'm on my way out to lunch. Can you take this one?"

Detective Sloane bit his bottom lip. "Send her over."

Samantha staggered to his desk. "Are you okay?" he asked her.

"I am ... considering what I've been through."

He rotated a pencil from the point to the eraser, a nervous habit he'd picked up over the years. "Now, in order for me to document the incident, we will go through the W's ... what, where, when—and you'll answer."

Samantha nodded and shards of leaves tumbled out of her messy hair. "Understood."

Detective Sloane nodded. "What happened?"

At that moment, she began to sob. "Someone grabbed my purse," sniffles intervened between sentences. "After a short struggle, he knocked me to my knees."

"I know you might not agree with me under these circumstances, but you're lucky. It could have gone differently. I'm sorry that happened to you, but in the future, don't fight with an assailant. You can replace a purse; your life is unreplaceable."

Detective Sloane tossed the file he was holding on top of the others in front of her, exposing a few sheets. "Now, let's move on to the other W's."

They did—extensively—and during that time, she couldn't help but peek at the first sheet of paper sticking out of the file. In the meantime, she described the assailant down to the scars on his face and wrist, something Detective Sloane appreciated. By the end of their discussion, their mood had lightened.

"If you have any questions, feel free to come in or give me a call." He gave her his card.

She looked at it and then at him. "Thank you. Actually, I do have a question."

"And that is?"

"The file you tossed—I noticed a familiar name on a list of some sort."

He retrieved the sheet of paper and looked at it. "Are you referring to this?" He showed it to her. "It's a missing person's log—which name are you referring to?"

"Bryson."

25

Hardly in a jesting mood, Uri opened the door, but with more force than necessary. Without warning, an object barreled toward him. It turned out that a large tree branch that hung over the cabin's roof broke, turning it into a makeshift battering ram that swayed into the structure. He deftly moved aside as it swung toward the door, narrowly avoiding it tearing into his gut.

"That was close," Uri let out a deep breath. "We should take care of it before it damages the structure or one of us."

Marc grabbed a part of the branch sticking out at the side as it swung away, yanked on it and the branch detached. They tossed it aside; Marc dusted his hands off, and entered the house with Uri trailing him. He went over to Tabitha and after carefully surveying her, Marc said, "You don't look so good. Are you okay?"

"I don't feel like myself, but other than being exhausted, I'm fine."

"All right. Let's call it a night." He held her hand and led her to the bedroom.

Long after they'd turned in for the night, Marc eased out of bed, being careful not to rouse her. He opened the front door, and ventured outdoors in the predawn hours to the woods, past the field to a clearing where he made a fire. He warmed his hands and stared deep into the flames, so deep that his vision blurred. Soon, a cloaked being emerged, holding a staff with a wolf's head for the handle while embers rose like fireflies outlining the cloak, creating a shadow that fizzled into a dull orange haze.

Marc sat alone against a tree stump surrounded by animalistic calls of the wild. All of a sudden, the critters went silent and whispers took over, invading his earlobes like sirens—warranting a reply, "I did," he said defiantly, "but what you're asking me to do—" A maddening glare emanated in his eyes. Marc shook his head. "No-no, I won't do it," he said pitifully.

26

The tall waves waned enough for the ship to brave the trip and before long, Draíocht Dol enlarged in the horizon, cultivating a ferocious gaze in his eyes. A paltry sum of five travelers braved the trip, two of whom felt nauseous and dizzy halfway there. Not long after their ill feelings began, the deck reeked of bile that didn't quite make it overboard. Thankfully, within the hour, they docked. Eager to escape the stench, Detective Sloane got off in a hurry and secured a ride out to the countryside.

Forty-five minutes later, he banged on the O'Brien's front door. "Is Uri in?" he asked, perhaps a little louder than necessary.

Tabitha opened the door with a cross look on her face. "Yes. Come in. Have a seat."

Detective Sloane entered and looked about the room. "On second thought, I'd like to speak with you first."

He skimmed through his notes. "Initially, you presumed that your husband perished during the flood. Is the same true for your son, Jon?"

A long, uncomfortable silence lingered before she responded. "He was killed moments before the wave hit," she said without giving it much thought.

Killed? Detective Sloane leafed through his pad in a hurry. "I don't recall you mentioning that he was killed before. Did you report the crime to the authorities?"

"I couldn't, even if I wanted to. Have you ever experienced or survived a Tsunami? If you had, you wouldn't ask that question. The wave swept us away; I was lost at sea for—only God knows how long and by the time I found my way home, I'd learned that the man responsible for my son's death died when the wave hit. With that said, reporting the crime to the authorities was the last thing on my mind."

Detective Sloane observed her body language down to the slightest twitch of her eye while he sat across from her. "How did Jon die?"

"One of Donovan's goons killed him." He had the urge to sport a maniacal grin, but contained himself and managed to keep a straight face.

"Mr. Kingsley sent two of his goons to encourage Marc to sell our crops to him, and when he refused, one of them, Anton, used Jon as a bargaining tool. Marc stood firm. He wasn't about to hand over our golden calf to a man who knows little about drudgery," her voice quivered.

Yes, Marc echoed that sentiment when we last spoke.

Now, tears seeped from her eyes. "Don't be fooled by his riches, he's as crooked as they come." Tabitha raised her gaze to meet his. Confident in her dramatization of the events, but by looking at her, there was no way for him to tell that a concealed smirk lay below the surface of her frown. *Yes, Detective Sloane, lap it up.*

Detective Sloane ground his teeth. "Before you go any further, help me to understand something ... Uri worked for Donovan at that time. Was he present when Jon was killed?"

"Yes ... he—was."

Detective Sloane's insides knotted as he voiced his next question. "I know Uri didn't know who he was. Did you?"

"Umm," she didn't know what to say, his question had caught her off guard. "He was on a horse—out by the entrance. I didn't get a good look at him," she said listlessly as she was drawn back to that moment. "That's why I didn't recognize him at that time.

"What kind of mother doesn't recognize her own son?" Sloane asked callously.

Disheartened by the lengths he was willing to go, Tabitha's eyes moistened. "Pardon me, Detective Sloane. I wasn't expecting my eldest son, whom I was told died while on his way to Astonia, to show up. There were more pressing matters at that time. One minute, I was pleading for Jon's life, and the next, I was holding his lifeless body in my arms, feral-eyed, angrier than I've ever been. After that, everything spiraled out of control. It wasn't until weeks later that I realized that he was alive, and there the day his brother died. Can you even begin to understand how devastated I was when I learned that?"

"I doubt it matters. You're the only person who can comprehend what that felt like."

"I beg to differ. Any humane person can."

"Maybe so, but that's not a part of my job description."

Marc entered the cabin. "What's he doing here?" His eyes traveled the room. "Where's Uri?"

"He's outside. Detective Sloane needed to speak with me in private."

"This is highly inappropriate—is he through?" his voice deepened.

"I'm here concerning police matters," he interrupted. "And no, I'm not finished. I have another question. Then, I'll have a word with your son."

Marc rested his hands on his hips and stood guard.

"Have you ever been to Vermouthshire? And before you answer that question, think long and hard."

"I was there the day before the nor'easter hit."

And there lies the *bow*, a long-awaited adrenaline rush. Sloane couldn't help himself; a thin smile surfaced.

"We went to buy clothing and other knick-knacks."

"I know," he said and Tabitha gulped. "I have a witness that places you there. Ironically, the same person also corroborated that you were also there on a previous occasion." He glanced at his notes, this time just for show. "You were also accompanied by a young man who's been identified as your son, Uri– Bryson—tomāto, tomädo." Detective Sloane swayed a dismissive hand.

Marc's breathing quickened. Unaware of the incident they were referring to, he found himself more invested in their conversation than he ought to be. Then again, he began to wonder why he had never made it a priority to learn more about what happened back home while he was marooned on the small island.

"I fail to see the significance," she said heatedly.

27

Detective Sloane grimaced. "That's all for now. Tell Uri that I'd like to speak with him," he said gruffly.

Tabitha nodded on her way out and made quick, angry strides while her face reddened. "Uri!" she called out.

He came out from the wooded area behind the house. After one look at her, he asked, "What's wrong?"

Tabitha folded her arms and turned away. "He wants to talk to you." Uri moved toward the door but stopped abruptly when she held his forearm. "Be careful, he's out for blood."

"I can handle him." Uri removed her hand, went inside and joined Detective Sloane at the dining table. Uri glared at him, "So, what is it this time?"

"There's been some new developments in the case, which relates to the disappearance of your former boss. Initially, you claimed not to know him, but then I learned that you worked for him."

"You're mistaken. You inquired about the business dealings my father had with him. So I answered accordingly," he clarified, clearly agitated.

"Yes, but hold on—" he glanced down at his notes again. "We've already established that you went by the name of Bryson."

Uri glared at Detective Sloane in a deer-like fashion for a while before answering.

"We've gone over this already—"

"I know," Detective Sloane said adamantly with a snide grimace, "but you don't get to decide the number of times I bring it up. When was the last time you worked for him?"

"Two—uh—maybe three weeks after the flood. I was injured, and hospitalized in St. Vincent's Hospital."

"How long were you there?"

"A week, maybe less."

"While you were there, did you meet anyone that you've stayed in contact with?"

"Not really …"

"Is that a yes or no?"

"Yes. I did."

"I'm assuming it's a woman. Is she a love interest?"

"Something like that—but we're just friends," he replied hesitantly.

Detective Sloane smirked. "On the last day that anyone can account for your former boss' whereabouts, you and your mother, who by the way previously said she had never stepped foot on Vermouthshire, were seen perusing the downtown area."

"And?" Uri exclaimed. "I'm sick and tired of these pointless questions." He felt like tipping the table but resisted the urge. "I haven't broken the law. If I had, I would be behind bars."

"That's not entirely true. Being an accomplice to a murder is a crime. Your brother was killed by Anton, the man you accompanied to this cabin." Sloane elaborated while tears fell from Uri's eyes.

"If I'd known what he planned to do, I wouldn't have come along." Now, an onslaught of tears fell with the timing of the second hand on a clock. "Can you imagine what it's like to wake up every day knowing that *I* brought death to my family's doorstep? I didn't pull the trigger, but that doesn't release me from guilt. I'll have to live with that for the rest of my life."

"No, I can't, but I wouldn't let the person responsible get away with murder, either."

"I doubt that's the case. The wave swept him away. I heard that scavengers feasted on his corpse before they found him. If that's true, I guess you could call it justice—karma. Whichever word suits your fancy."

Sloane's stare intensified. "Your former coworkers: the butler, cook, driver, and housekeeper, were all presumed missing. When did you last see them?"

"The day, I quit. I saw the butler and driver on the way in. I tendered my resignation and left."

"I think that'll do it," Sloane dusted his coat as he got up. "I'll be on my way, but don't get too comfortable. The next time we meet, I'll have matching bracelets for you and your mother," he said wearing a thin smile that wavered on his way out.

28

Cold sweat seeped from the base of her neck and forehead as Tabitha held on to the tree and spat out what was left of the rancid taste in her mouth. After regaining composure, she came out from behind the house and wiped her mouth. Marc noticed her as he came from the opposite direction, dropped the tool from his hand, and ran to her. He held her close.

"You're so pale, and look like you're on the verge of passing out. Should I send for the doctor?"

"That's not—necessary," she paused midsentence as a gag reflex took hold. Seconds later, vomit projected from her gaped mouth. Marc held her and walked her to the cabin.

"I'll send Uri to get the doctor," he said as they sat side by side on the bed.

Tabitha placed her hand atop his, "It's not necessary, at least not yet."

"Have you seen yourself lately?" he asked, wearing worry lines.

"I'm pregnant," she blurted out.

He turned abruptly, "Pregnant?"

At the age of forty-two, it was the last thing she'd expected. "I assumed I had caught a virus that I couldn't shake—," she rubbed her stomach, "until today when I felt it move inside me. By my calculation, I'm three months along." Tabitha stifled a laugh, but oddly, a tear fell.

Marc held her hand. "The child will be warmly welcomed. We didn't plan to have any more children, but it's a blessing. The sound of young children in a house adds a special quality to a home."

"I agree, but when Jon comes to mind ... my heart aches."

"Understandably, but this child is not his replacement, it's an addition to our family." Marc gently kissed her on the side of her temple. "Everything will work out, you'll see. But, for now, get some rest." He stood, and strode to the doorway with the gait of a weary man. Each step taken was heavier than the last and when he arrived at the threshold, he looked back at her and closed the door.

29

With daylight fading around them, Uri stocked the crops harvested earlier that day in the shed. During that time, he and Marc discussed the profitability of Thursdays, which typically brought in the most clientele. The idea of opening at first light seemed doable, but it warranted an early morning trip to the pier, which thrilled neither of them. Despite what the task entailed, Uri volunteered.

After they hashed that out, Marc retreated to the confines of their cabin, where he warmly watched over Tabitha. They talked as he sat at her bedside and shared the following day's plans. At some point down the line, her eyes grew heavy even though she tried to fight it, but eventually, she succumbed to sleep.

Tabitha laid in bed with the covers up to her neck alternating between sleep and being barely awake, stirring, sweating, yearning, only to slip deeper into an abyss where time held no precedence. In the tepid, alien environment, mist skulked along the ground, immersing her and everything it met in the secluded wooded area. Tabitha frantically turned in place, hoping to find a way out. Meanwhile, something at the center of the dizzying expanse caught her eye.

A distorted sphere hovered six feet above and warped like clay molding on a potter's wheel, held in place by a headless body engulfed in tumultuous blue flames. The apex fashioned itself into a human head, although one side of its face sank. *No,* it sagged, even as the guise continued to define itself. At that point, the flesh fell away from the tissue exposing facial muscles, which resembled dried meat–only softer, with the raw side up, freeing a lurid, burgundy liquid that embodied a sickening metallic odor. In the background, a prominent malefic tree stood out as its henchmen. Creeping vines with innumerable tendrils increased tenfold and extended well beyond the trunk, slithering beneath the mist loud enough for her to hear them close in on her.

Before she knew it, they scaled her legs, waist, and crown, preparing her for a mummified death.

Paralyzed and shrouded in darkness—the unwavering, indeterminate totality of it—she wept. *Just breathe, it's not real,* she told herself even as the vines fashioned themselves into a taut lariat around her neck, siphoning her breath. Soon air clogged her ears and induced a disorienting silence that quickly turned noisy as the beat of her heart echoed in her ear. By that point, minuscule balls of floating white light invaded her vision, which grew narrower by the second. Now, her heart beat faintly, jaws slackened, and the world darkened.

Tabitha awoke in a febrile state, drenched, breathing like she'd run around the island twice. She flinched as her stomach tightened and clutched the sheets in her fists. Her wheezed breaths fogged the air for the next few minutes until the feeling passed.

"Marc," she cried out. "Uri," she yelled for even louder, but then she recalled that he'd opted to spend the night at the store.

Another round of contractions was upstaged by her shrilling cries. "Marc," she hollered in between gasps, "where are you?" She stopped abruptly and considered the current hour–between midnight and sunrise—it dawned on her where Marc might be. She bared her teeth in a peeled grimace as the pains resurfaced.

•••

Meanwhile outside, slivers of light merged with the horizon, chasing the dark, lighting the atmosphere even as he lay by the fire, eyes wild, mouth muffled by villainous vines that also bound his feet. Only then did he realize that his role as an emissary was a grave mistake, fating him to follow its commands, and when he didn't, this was the consequence.

Even though he was deep in the woodland, Marc heard Tabitha's cries. In the clearing barely lit by the fading moon, Marc watched as his captor coolly walked away. Having an idea of his destination brought a sense of urgency that increased as he heard Tabitha call out for him again. Marc wiggled his way out of his restraints, pulled the vines away and flung them aside. He sprinted ahead, caught up with, and tackled his captor, knocking him to the ground. They tumbled ruthlessly, punching, kicking, and thrusting each other up against trees until they were awash in each other's sweat.

At least, that was the case until one of them drew back a fisted hand and landed a blow that sent the recipient spinning into an extended branch that knocked him off his heels. The other man took off, running toward the cabin. Rebounding quickly, he jumped to his feet and took off after him.

Marc ran with a sense of urgency to the cabin but then stopped abruptly, wiped the blood from the corner of his lip, tapped dirt off his clothing, and jogged on. Not long afterward, he came through the entryway like a ruffian coming for payback, only to see his wife in the throes of what appeared to be an intolerable pain.

"What's wrong?" he asked, feigning calmness.

"I—" was all she managed to say before an additional round of contractions came. A succession of rapid breaths trailed it. "I'm in labor," Tabitha blurted it out and dug her nails into the mattress.

She tolerated it as best she could and when the ache subsided, she lay there taking shallow breaths, gazing at him with a dull look in her eyes.

30

After fifteen pain-free minutes had passed, she grasped his hand.

"You should stay in bed, dear."

"I'm—fine," she assured, breathily with an air of uncertainty.

Marc helped Tabitha up from the bed. Just then, a heavy thud was heard and the door swung open. He charged Marc, bringing their brawl that had long ago turned ugly, indoors. Marc shielded Tabitha from the lunatic who was trying to grab her.

"What do you want-t-t?" Marc slurred. "Get out-t-t," he yelled in a dragging snarl.

He chucked the intruder in the chest, a motion that sent him stumbling backward into Tabitha and sent the intruder in the opposite direction.

At a loss for words, she eased away from them to the safety of the kitchen in a composed panic. Within the short glimpses she caught of him, Tabitha noticed similarities between them as they tussled each other to a dizzying pace, knocking over everything they encountered until one of them fell. At that point, Marc straddled *Marc*, pinning him down with his weight and put his hands around Marc's neck.

"How does that feel?" he asked through partly clenched teeth as their eyes locked in a rabid stare.

With her back to the counter, and waist pressed against the edge, one arm lay still at her side, and the other behind her, while fragments of her nightmare invaded her mind's eye. Creeping vines scaled her, bound her. *Breathe ... breathe,* her inner voice instructed. Just then, a chair tumbled away from the scuffle and hit her, freeing her from the trance.

Marc pinned the other Marc to the floor while he fought to pry him off. The Marc that was on top stumbled toward Tabitha as her heart beat like the footfalls of a Trojan horse, so much so that it was all she could hear. Another frame from her horrific visualizations pierced her and came into focus. Facial muscles cured to jerky, although blood—plenty of it—made it supple, and blue flames, the rising mist— back to Marc again—running toward her. Just inches from her, sunlight filtered through the window, filling her eyes.

"Run," he said through a crazed sneer, "get as far away from—"

Fearsome eyes glared back at him as her hand forcefully plowed into him, interrupting him mid-sentence as she delivered a menacing blow. His eyes bulged as she withdrew her instrument, he looked down at the blood-smeared knife as it came loose from his gut just in time for her to plunge it into him again. He fell into her, his head slipping alongside her as he lifelessly slumped down her leg to the floor.

All it took was a nudge of her knee and he fell down on the ground with a dull thud. The linear line of blood expanded as his wounds gushed, saturating his shirt, and spilled onto the floor, forming an island of blood. A faint, gurgled hitch came from his loose lips. He looked dauntlessly past her and released a final breath.

An ill-tempered expression convened on the other Marc's face. Then, he dragged the tip of his tongue across his teeth. "How does it feel?" He circled her like a conqueror, knowing deep down that he'd outwitted her. Tabitha looked up at him. "To be fair, I'll give you some time to process this," he explained in a condescending way. Now at a standstill, the depth of his voice began to change, and then softened to an effeminate tone. "Then again, I'll show you." His dark, cold stare bore right through her.

Dumbfounded, Tabitha reacted, "What are you talking about? What have I ever done to you for you to treat me this way?" She queried angrily and then she looked away.

Prideful, Marc glanced at the body on the floor for some time. His lips stiffened and then spread into a pompous smile. "You've done plenty, Tabitha O'Brien, but you needn't worry, my work here is done," and with that said, he wiped his hands.

Her fiery gaze returned to him. Once again, Tabitha's dream—but this time, all of it—replayed in a quick recap, and upon its completion, her vision cleared. It was then that she got a better look at him, but by then, his sinew had gradually melted away like molten rock.

Unbeknownst to her, Marc had made a deal with the cloaked being while he was a castaway on that spit of land, and its terms—wagering his life, for his soul—linked him thereafter to the transcendent being.

At first, Marc probably thought he was hallucinating, but it didn't take long for him to learn otherwise. Additionally, the cloaked image Marc encountered on that deserted island and the Marc standing before her were one and the same.

He unraveled before her very eyes like a venomous flower that took centuries to bloom; its layers falling to the wayside like a dense pile of slick seaweed. At the end of its shedding, an opaque figure remained, and it was none other than Cora Kingsley, Albert's wife, adding the final dressing to her crafty requite. It was all her doing from the start. She resurrected a corpse, made it a creature of her own design, originating from the depths of Turtle Pond, and fashioned it into her tool for revenge. Once her experiment cured, she manipulated it, groomed it to liken him. Then she joined the mold, bonding herself to it and gave it purpose for as long as Marc drew breath.

"Just so you know, I was the one who came when you needed him. If only for that reason, you should be grateful that I comforted you," Cora added while rays of sunlight immersed her.

"All your husband had to do was kill you. That's all, but he refused, so I improvised," she complained. "Though I must admit, this outcome was more gratifying. Now, do you get it?" Cora jibed, softening her voice as if she were speaking to a child.

Alas, the knife fell from Tabitha's grasp as she slumped to the floor. "Yes," Tabitha replied dully. Reduced to a vacant stare, she observed as Cora, in all of ten seconds, diminished to a blur of color. But before she dissipated, she divulged the final jab, "An eye for an eye, a husband for a husband." With that said, she was gone.

A vitriolic look spread in Tabitha's eyes. Disarmed by the nature of Cora's crafty redress, she surrendered to quivering cries fed by an unspeakable anguish that evolved into frantic wails, and when there were no tears left to shed, she reached for Marc's hand and held it.

Even though she was free of Cora, Tabitha stayed in the same spot well into the afternoon, lost in thought to the point that she hadn't heard when a wagon entered the yard or when Detective Sloane called out for her. Sloane approached the cabin and passed the threshold. From the doorway, he saw her sitting on the floor at the center of the kitchen and dining area holding Marc's hand.

His eyes closed briefly as he felt his innards recoil. He'd spent most of the morning going over all of the information he'd compiled with Sergeant Pistone, after which the sergeant came to a maddening conclusion. Even though Mr. Kingsley and his staff may very well be dead, there was no evidence: no blood, no bodies or indications of foul play to support that a crime was committed, let alone to make an arrest.

Sergeant Pistone let out a pillaging breath. "Bring her in anyhow," he said with a dismissive wave of his hand.

Shortly after their meeting, Detective Sloane had left for Draíocht Dol, hoping this voyage would be more hospitable. Instead, he was subjected to this morbid scene.

"Wha…What happened?" he stuttered. Tabitha lifted her head, putting her tear-stricken eyes on display. "I killed him."

Detective Sloane ambled a short distance to reach her, but it felt like a mile. "Tabitha O'Brien, you're under arrest for the murder of Marc O'Brien," he started and sighed. "I came out here to escort you to Vermouthshire … we needed a formal statement concerning Jon's death."

Conflicted, Detective Sloane shook his head as he reflected on his long-held belief that when—*if* the moment came, he'd be thrilled to make an arrest and close the case, but he wasn't. Tabitha looked innocuously ahead as he fettered one hand and then the other behind her back while he read her her Miranda Rights. He traveled over to the bed, removed the sheet, and covered Marc's body.

"He'll be taken care of, I promise. It's the least I can do," he vowed and bowed his head. Nothing he said registered; she continued to stare at the thickening formation of blood on the floor.